KEEPERS

KEEPERS

Treasure-Hunt Poems

JOHN FRANK

Photographs by
KEN ROBBINS

A NEAL PORTER BOOK
ROARING BROOK PRESS
NEW YORK

For Dee and Lisa
—J.F.

Text copyright © 2008 by John Frank
Illustrations copyright © 2008 by Ken Robbins
A Neal Porter Book
Published by Roaring Brook Press
Roaring Brook Press is a division of Holtzbrinck Publishing
Holdings Limited Partnership
175 Fifth Avenue, New York, New York 10010
All rights reserved
www.roaringbrookpress.com

Distributed in Canada by H. B. Fenn and Company, Ltd.

Library of Congress Cataloging-in-Publication Data
Frank, John.
Keepers : treasure-hunt poems / by John Frank ;
photographs by Ken Robbins. — 1st ed.
p. cm.
"A Neal Porter book."
ISBN-13: 978-1-59643-197-3   ISBN-10: 1-59643-197-0
I. Robbins, Ken, ill.   II. Title.
PS3556.R33425K44 2008   811'.54—dc22
2007013201

Roaring Brook Press books are available for special promotions and premiums.
For details, contact: Director of Special Markets, Holtzbrinck Publishers.

Printed in China
Book design by Jennifer Browne
First edition April 2008
2 4 6 8 10 9 7 5 3 1

CONTENTS

Foreword

I. AT THE BEACH

Low Tide   11

Glass Jewel   12

After the Storm   14

Abalone Shell   17

Driftwood Bird   19

Turritella Shell   20

II. IN THE ATTIC

A Trunk of Clothes   23

Doll   27

Globe   29

Baseball Cards   30

Medal   32

Music Box   34

III. IN THE MOUNTAINS AND DESERT

Geode   37

Desert Rose   38

Prospecting   39

Rattle   40

Tourmalines   41

Fossil   43

IV. AT THE FLEA MARKET

Die-cast Cars   47

Stamps   48

Comic Book   49

Puppets   51

Model Train   52

Costume Jewelry   53

V. BENEATH THE GROUND

Time Machine   57

Old Coin   59

Point   61

Pottery Jar   62

Necklace   63

Hole   64

The wonder of treasure. It makes us say *Wow*. It's the gleam of a gold nugget, or the fire in a precious gem. It's the geometry of an unusual seashell, or the craftsmanship of a fine antique. It's the death of an animal, preserved in a fossil—or the birth of a legend, preserved in a baseball card. It's the step from the rarely valuable . . . to the valuably rare.

And to treasure collectors, how rare an object seems can determine whether it's worthwhile to collect. If fossils and beautiful seashells were piled high in our backyard, we probably wouldn't bother to display any of them proudly inside our home. If diamonds and rubies lined every street, few of us would wish to wear them around our fingers and wrists and neck. And if Babe Ruth had autographed a million baseballs, well, we might still be using some of them to play catch.

But the Babe *didn't* sign a million baseballs. Only a few bearing his signature are around today. They're rare—beyond the ordinary. (Extraordinary, you might say.) So if you're someone who collects autographs of baseball players, a ball signed by Babe Ruth is a treasure you'd love to have. (And you'd be crazy to play catch with one. Can you imagine dropping it in the mud?)

Here's something else to consider about treasure. Suppose you did own one of those rare baseballs. Would *how* you came to own it affect your feelings about it? If you were rich and had bought it from an expensive dealer, would you cherish it as much as if you had found it yourself in an attic or a flea market? Or suppose you collected fossils instead of autographed baseballs. Would handing someone a wad of cash for the tooth of a *Tyrannosaurus rex* excite you as much as digging out that tooth from the desert?

Perhaps not. For many of us, simply paying lots of money for rare objects seldom feels as rewarding as searching for and discovering those objects on our own. There's a well-known phrase: the thrill of the hunt. Couple that with the joy of discovery, and you've got a feeling that's tough to beat. Finding a scarce penny while sorting through a jar of change, happening upon an exquisite seashell while combing the shore, stumbling across a famous artist's painting while poking through the clutter in a junk shop—these are moments that make our heart race and take our breath away. They're treasure's greatest pleasure.

—J.F.

I. AT THE BEACH

LOW TIDE

Polished stones,
And old bleached bones,
And shells like broken lockets
Lie scattered on the sandy shore
Where the ocean empties its pockets.

GLASS JEWEL

Once you were
just broken glass,
but years of
sea on sand

turned you to
the teardrop jewel
I now hold
in my hand.

AFTER THE STORM

Heed the days
when the swell is raised
by the winds that a storm sets free,
for that's when the past
onto shore is cast
from the ships that have braved the sea.

A watchful eye,
with luck might spy,
in a tangle of seaweed strands,
a flask or jar,
years old, from afar,
come to rest on the coastal sands,

or a net's glass float,

torn adrift from its boat,

when a fish haul was dragged on deck . . .

or a coin of gold

from the cargo hold

of a long-lost Spanish wreck.

ABALONE SHELL

Rocking
in the current's swirl . . .
a melted rainbow
cupped in pearl.

DRIFTWOOD BIRD

This
piece of branch
from a fallen tree

was
sculpted wings
by the churning sea,

brought
back to land
by the waves' long reach,

left
poised to fly
from the windy beach.

TURRITELLA SHELL

A wave's white mane
shook free this horn—
the spiraled crown
of a unicorn.

II. IN THE ATTIC

A TRUNK OF CLOTHES

As I lift the lid of a battered trunk,
the smell of oldness fills my nose,
a whiff of dust and mothballs
wafting up from layers of curious clothes—

a red bow tie with polka dots,
a striped sport coat, a lacy wrap,
a pair of gloves a half yard long,
a gold purse with a beaded strap,

some stretchy gray suspenders,
an embroidered skirt, and—*ooh la la*—
a pair of long pink panties and,
in matching pink, a mountainous bra,

an overcoat of camel hair,
a rhinestone blouse, a scarf of plaid,
a velvet gown, an old tuxedo—
clothes grandparents might have had

before they were grandparents.
Did people actually wear this stuff?
I ask myself as I pull out
a two-tone shoe, a fur-trimmed muff,

a hat that's so old-fashioned
you would not be caught dead dressed in it . . .
but then, I glance behind me,
and . . . I wonder if . . . it just might fit.

I try it on, then make my way

to a mirror hung in an oval rim;

I tilt the frame, blow off the dust,

then grasp the hat and bend its brim

and shape the crown, and tug and lift,

this way and that, till above my brow

the hat sets right, and I give the glass

a long hard look . . . I'm *stylin'* now.

DOLL

I spot you in a wooden cradle,
tucked beneath a tiny spread—
a square of cloth a girl might once
have worn for warmth about her head.

I touch your rounded porcelain face
and wonder, Were you left behind
by someone who grew tired of you?
Or hidden here for me to find?

GLOBE

A winter frozen in a dome of glass . . .
I pick it up and turn it upside down,
then put it back and watch it come to life. . . .
It's snowing, now, upon the little town.

BASEBALL CARDS

A shoe box full of baseball cards,
of players from olden days,
with tiny batting averages
and giant E.R.A.'s—
an absolutely sorry stack,
not worth the gum once in each pack,
but . . . what is this? . . .
A rookie *Willie Mays?*

The "Say-Hey Kid"? The legend
of the one-hand basket catch?
There was no fly he couldn't field,
no base he couldn't snatch,
no juicy pitch he couldn't clout,
no runner he could not throw out—
his glove and speed and power
had no match!

BO JACKSON

ROYALS·LF

And, what? A *Sandy Koufax*??
Once the greatest arm of all,
he threw so hard that if you blinked
you wouldn't see the ball;
the batters always swung too late,
they'd miss the lightning sear the plate,
then hear the umpire's thunderous
"Stee-rike!" call.

And, yes! A *Henry Aaron*,
baseball's longtime home-run king!
He belted seven fifty-five
with his colossal swing!
His bat was money in the bank!
A MINT-CONDITION HAMMERIN' HANK!
I wouldn't trade these cards
for anything!

MEDAL

You must be the medal
they pinned
on his uniform—

bronze,
with a ribbon
of red, white, and blue.

I read of that war.
To this day
Grandpa still will not

speak much
about what he did—
but you do.

MUSIC BOX

I twist the box's windup key,
and when I raise the top, I see,
below a plate of beveled glass,
a turning cylinder of brass
with tiny pins that seem to know,
like fingers trained, which of the row
of notes to play—which teeth within
the metal comb to plink. Each pin
awaits its turn so patiently
to help create the melody.

III. IN THE MOUNTAINS AND DESERT

GEODE

I cracked a stone egg
dark as smoke,
and found, inside,
a crystal yolk
as purple as
a sheet of sky
pulled over twilight's
closing eye.

DESERT ROSE

For thousands of years
you've slowly grown
and stayed in bloom—
a rose of stone.

PROSPECTING

I dip my pan beneath the stream
where twisting currents glide,
and scoop a layer of gravel bed
and shake it side to side:
among those tiny rocks, I know,
gold flakes and nuggets hide.

RATTLE

A tiny rattle
lay hidden in
a papery crinkle
of shed snakeskin.

TOURMALINES

I'm foraging for tourmalines,
transparent yellows, pinks, and greens,
glass miniatures of ruins of old
whose toppled pillars once stood bold.

FOSSIL

Far from where
the breaking salt-tide moans,
a rock I find
reveals the past to me—
the outline of
an ocean creature's bones:

these hills must once
have stood beneath the sea.

IV. AT THE FLEA MARKET

DIE-CAST CARS

Eyes cast for die-cast
cars for my collection,
up and down the rows I pace,
scouring the swap meet's sprawling space
for rare *Hot Wheels*
and *Matchbox* deals,
those sweet hot rods I dream I race—
no bargain here will slip past
my detection.

STAMPS

Stamps from all around the world,
too valuable to mail,
each one a tiny work of art
behind which lies a tale.

COMIC BOOK

Good ol' Clark Kent,
that mild-mannered reporter,
on sale at a swap meet,
a buck and a quarter.

Not bad for a comic
in decent condition—
I wish, though, that it were
a mint first-edition.

PUPPETS

Wanted: actors
from every different land,
the kind who won't perform
without a friend to lend a hand,

the kind who'll let me guide them
as upon the stage they walk,
and let my voice be theirs
whenever it's their turn to talk.

And whether led by rod or string
or worn as if a glove,
ascending as a shadow
or paraded from above,

some will, I hope, be eager
to come home with me today,
to be part of my puppet troupe
when I put on my play.

MODEL TRAIN

An old-time locomotive painted black,
a steam dome and a sandbox on its back,
a steel-wheeling,
engine-chugging,
brake-squealing,
freight car-tugging,
bell-clanging,
coal-reeking,
boiler-banging,
whistle-shrieking,
grinding, growling,
midnight-howling,
puffing, chuffing,
steep hill-huffing
belcher-of-black-smoke-out-of-its-stack—

I want that locomotive for my track.

COSTUME JEWELRY

Make-believe diamonds and rubies and emeralds
in make-believe-gold bracelets, pendants, and rings,
make-believe silver and opal and sapphire—
for make-believe queens
and their make-believe kings.

V. BENEATH THE GROUND

TIME MACHINE

My shovel and hoe

are a time

machine

Taking me

into the

past

The farther I

dig through

the soil

below

The earlier back

through the

years I

go

As older and

older the

artifacts

grow

Each deeper

in time

than the

last.

OLD COIN

I found a dime
a century old
while digging deep below.

Imagine what
it might have bought
a hundred years ago.

POINT

This point of chipped stone,
edges notched on each side,
to the shaft of an arrow
or spear was once tied,
and aimed at a beast
for its meat and its hide.

POTTERY JAR

Born from clay and fire,
worn to shards
by time and weather,

this spill of
puzzle pieces waits
to be joined back together.

NECKLACE

Drilled shells and teeth,
now scattered like seeds:
a primitive necklace's
elegant beads.

HOLE

With all my strength upon my spade
I dug a secret hole,
One so deep and dark
Not even gopher, shrew, or mole
Would dare come near, for fear
That they might lose their earthen floor
And slip into the still, black depth
And fall forever more.

I then gathered all my things
That wink with borrowed light—
Buttons, pennies, bits of glass—
And buried them that night.
Ancient treasures, years from now,
Await the curious soul
Who lifts a spade and splits the ground
And finds my secret hole.